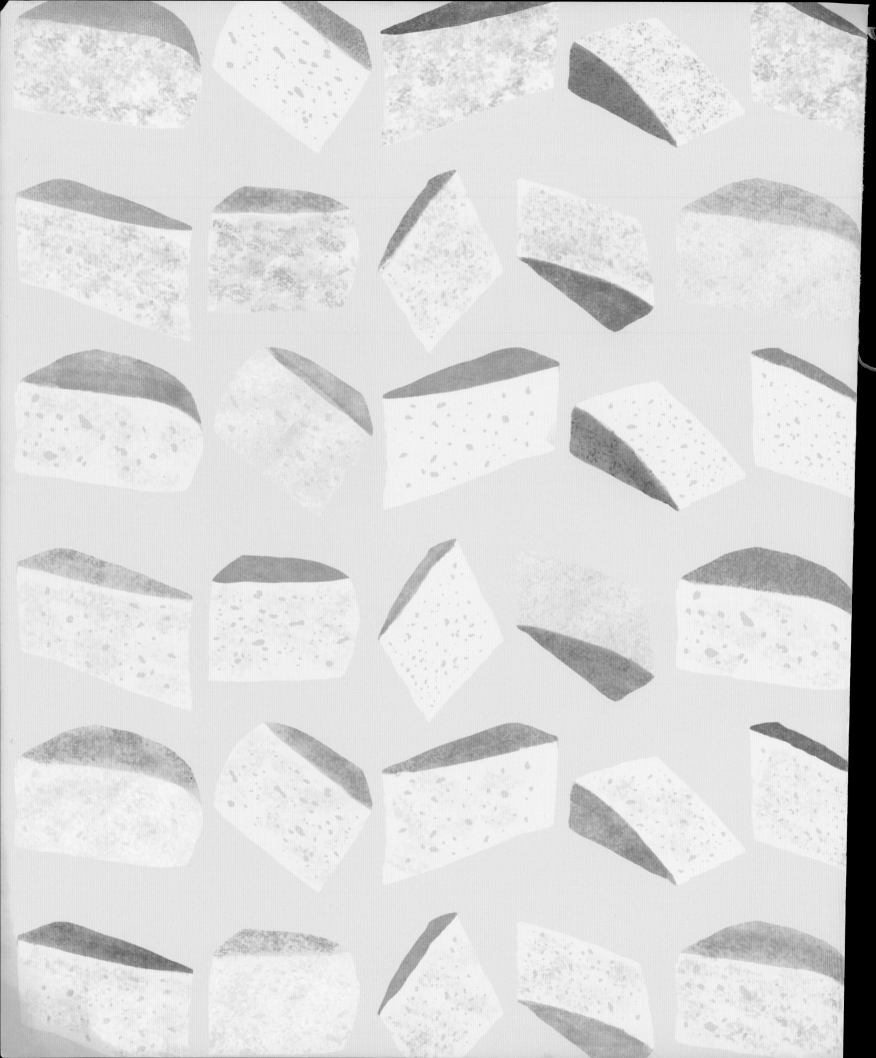

For Lucy, Pete, Meg, Jake and Will — L.R.
For Pirate Jess and the two shipmates, Laura and Emily — M.C.

First published 2017 by Macmillan Children's Books
an imprint of Pan Macmillan
20 New Wharf Road, London N1 9RR
Associated companies throughout the world
www.panmacmillan.com

ISBN: 978-1-5290-2786-0

1 3 5 7 9 8 6 4 2

A CIP catalogue record for this book is
available from the British Library.

Printed in China

PIRATE PETE
and his
SMELLY FEET

LUCY ROWLAND   MARK CHAMBERS

MACMILLAN CHILDREN'S BOOKS

Old Pirate Pete had the smelliest feet,
The cheesiest feet on the sea!

Each time he walked by
All his shipmates would cry,

"What a bad STINK! Deary me!"

The captain and crew
didn't know *what* to do,

They liked to keep tidy and neat.

For though they looked mean,
They were really quite clean,

And they'd all had enough of Pete's feet!

They found a big tub and they gave Pete a scrub,
But the water turned murky and black.

It didn't take long
'Til they noticed the pong

And they realised the smell had come back.

The captain said, "Crew, there's just one thing to do,
It's time that Old Pete walked the plank."

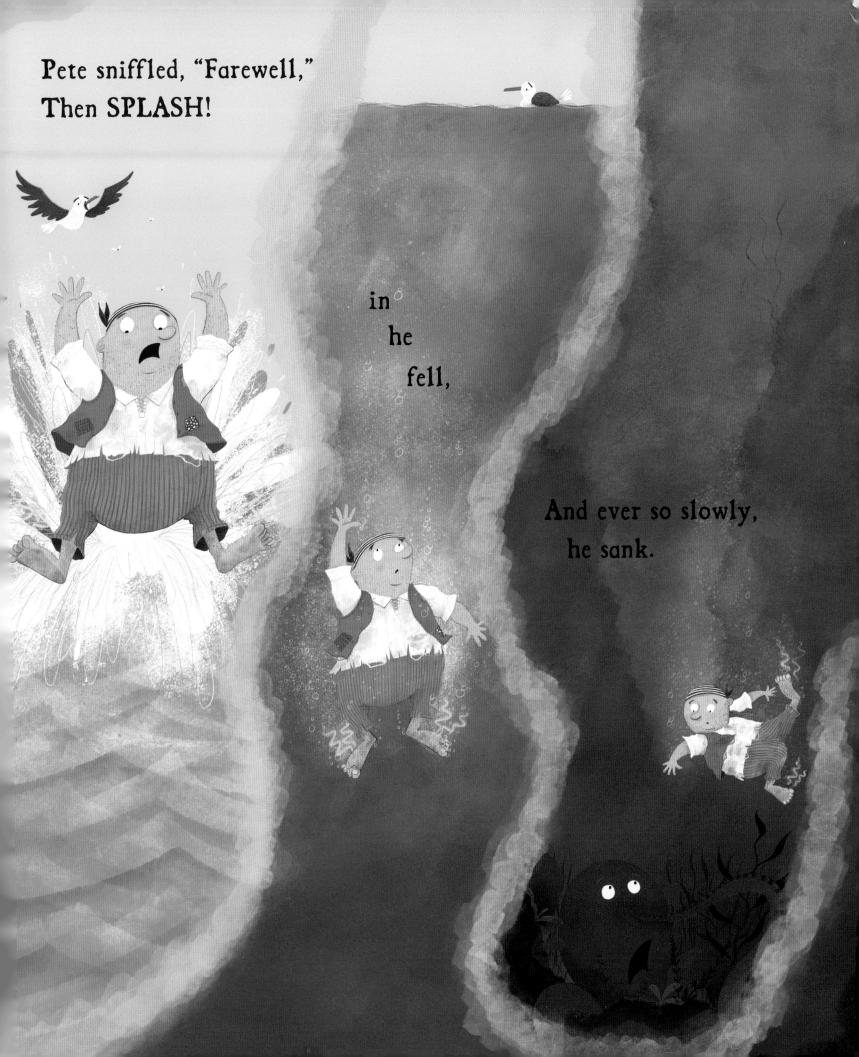

Pete sniffled, "Farewell,"
Then SPLASH!

in
he
fell,

And ever so slowly,
he sank.

The seaweed, it swirled round Pete's feet, as he whirled
Through the sea with a

SWOOSH!

and a SWISH!

He turned a bit pink
When his terrible stink
Disturbed all the poor little fish!

By the time he found land, Pete was covered in sand,

He stomped through the leaves and the dirt.

He squelched through some tar

And he wandered so far

That even his toenails hurt!

But then came a YELP! Someone calling for help,
Old Pirate Pete looked around.

He heard, "Help us, please!"
As he looked to the seas,
"My friends are in trouble," he frowned.

And there by the boat, which was barely afloat,
Were three hungry sharks in a row!

The pirates looked pale
As they clung to the sail,

And the sharks circled slowly below.

Old Pete scratched his head, "I must help them!" he said,

The pirates looked close to defeat.

Just then . . . from the sea . . .
Came a strong pong of Brie
And the captain called out,

"LOOK, IT'S PETE!"

Pete's feet caked in tar
could be smelt from afar,
But the pirates just shouted, "Hooray!"

'Cause the sharks took one sniff
Of that terrible whiff,

"Iv

And they turned and swam quickly away!

Standing slightly upwind, the pirates all grinned,
"Three cheers for Pete's foul-smelling feet!"

From then on, the crew,
And the young captain too,
Weren't nearly so clean or so neat.

And if sharks were around, then the crew could be found
Wafting their toes in the breeze.

They'd wink at Old Pete
As they scrubbed, head to feet . . .

WITH HANDFULS OF STINKY OLD CHEESE!

"Can you find the sock hidden on each double page?"